The Magic Christmas Box

"Package for T. Jay Toucan!" said the mailman.

"That's me!" T. Jay said. He grabbed the package. "Why, it's from my cousin who lives in the North Pole — P. Jay Penguin. He's sent me a Christmas present. His presents are always strange and different."

T. Jay ripped the brown paper off the package.

"What did you get?" asked Alec Alligator as he walked up to his friend, T. Jay. T. Jay read the postcard that came with the present:

Dear Cousin T. Jay, I am giving you this Magic Christmas Box for Christmas. Shake the box, and it will grant you a wish. Love, Cousin P. Jay. P.S. The Magic Christmas Box will grant you only two wishes. Enjoy!'

T. Jay's friends gathered around him. "Help me decide what to wish for, my friends."

"Look at all the snow in the North Pole," said Alec Alligator looking at the picture on the postcard. "Why doesn't it ever snow in the jungle for Christmas?"

"Yes," cried the other jungle animals. "We want snow! We want this to be a real Christmas."

"That sounds like a wonderful idea!" said T. Jay. He shook the box.

"Magic Christmas Box, we want snow for this Christmas season!"

"Look," Alec Alligator said. "Snowflakes! It's starting to snow!"

"Let it snow! Let it snow!" they sang, as the snowflakes began to fall faster and faster.

"Let's build a snowman!" said T. Jay Toucan. "Snow fight! Snow fight!" yelled the jungle animals as they made snowballs and threw them at each other.

Later, when T. Jay decided to fly to a tree limb, he found he could not get off the ground.

"My wings!" he cried. "They're frozen! I can't fly!"

Alec Alligator walked home for some lunch.

"Where is my swamp home?" he asked himself.

Then he realized what had happened.

"My home!" he cried. "It's frozen over."

Sara Zebra slipped and fell on the slippery snow and ice.

"Wow," she said, "this snow stuff is hard to walk on."

"I'm cold!" said Tees Tiger.

"I'm not cold," said Milo Monkey. "I'm freezing!"

The animals complained and whined about the cold.

"Do something, T. Jay," they pleaded. "Tell your magic box to take the snow away!"

"There is only one wish left," said T. Jay. "I guess we will have to use it only one way."

T. Jay shook the box. "Magic Christmas Box, take the snow away from here!"

The snow melted just in time for the Annual Jungle Christmas Party.

"This turned out to be the best Christmas ever!" said Alec Alligator.

"Yes," said T. Jay. "It's not snow that makes Christmas. It's being together with your friends!"

And then the jungle animals opened presents and sang Christmas carols.